written by
Barbara Joosse

Please Is a Good Word to Say

illustrated by
Jennifer Plecas

Philomel Books

For Maaike B. Tyke, because you live your life with humor, warmth and courage.　—Maman

For goops everywhere.　—J.P.

Please

is a good word to say.

When you say it,
it puts a smile on your words.

I try to say please one single time,
like this:

I try not to say it a lot of times, like this:

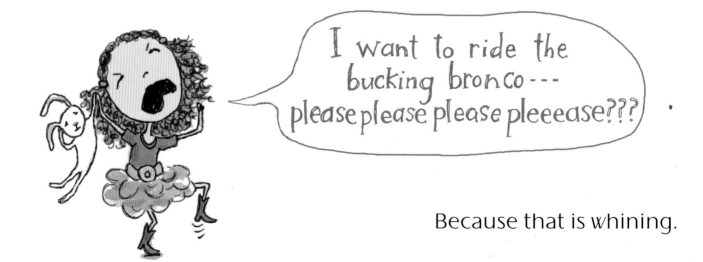

Because that is whining.

I also try not to say please and grab
at the same time.

Because that is bossy.

One of my best words is

Thank You.

Thank you, sun, for dancing through my window
and pluffy air for waking up my nose.

Thank you, fuzzy slippers,
which are pillows on my feet,

and thank you thank you thank you
for my oatmeal, Mama,
just like I like it with butter and brown sugar and nuts.
Oh I am so happy with my oatmeal
which is having a party on my tongue that I must say

Thank you!

This word is no trouble at all to say
because it makes everybody happy.

Here is what I think:

You can say thank you with a hug

and then, if you want to, you can say it
out loud at the same time.

Then thank you is like a double-dip ice cream
cone, because it's twice as nice.

I'm sorry is a good trouble word.

I say it when I get too fighty.

For example, Lydia was painting her toes with ruby
sparkle polish.
Which I love.
So I said nicely,

May **I** polish my
toes, too, please?

And Lydia said,

Maybe later, Harriet,
if there's any left.

And then she used up all the polish.

So
I smudged her sparkle with my foot
and Lydia cried.
Well, I was sorry,
mostly.
So then it's a good thing to say . . .

Excuse me is another trouble word.

I know that my mouth

or tummy

or butt

shouldn't make gross sounds
like burping or gurgling or you-know-what.
But sometimes they do.

I know that I shouldn't chew with my mouth
open because people can see the
mashed-up food inside.

But sometimes I do.

Then I say

And it makes the trouble better.

There are other words that make
this world nice.

Usually, your own name,

when you say it at just the right time.

When the phone rings, I answer it like this:

Hello, this is Harriet.

Then people know who I am.

If I want to double-dip a phone hello, I say:

Hello, this is Harriet. May I help you?

Whenever I say "May I help you?"

I feel like Super Harriet.

Oh it is so especially nice
to make someone feel good with your words.
So I try to say I like something whenever I can.

For example:

I really like your party shoes, Grammie. I like the dazzles on them and I also like the bows. They are soooooo fancy.

Almost everyone likes to be

fancy

For another example:

I like this painting, Rosie. I like the colors in it and I like the zebra.

Mama says I should say I like something
only when I really mean it.

Here's a funny thing about words.
Sometimes you should absolutely positively talk.
And sometimes you shouldn't.

>When someone asks a question,
> or says hello,
>you should answer back.
>Even if you're shy.

You don't have to say a lot of words, just a few.

When someone else is talking,
  you should be quiet until they're finished.
Even if they talk a very long time.

Oh, you should have seen it! First, I jumped up and then I turned around a bunch of times and then this big giant thing came and it was stomping STOMP! STOMP! STOMP! And then I jumped! And then I ran behind the big wall and then... you should have seen it!

Now I'll sing a thank-you song to you.

Oh I like you so much for listening to my very polite words:
Like please and thank you.
Like I'm sorry and excuse me.
Like my name and may I help you!

These words were so fun to say and sing sing Sing Sing!
AND! I wish this song would be forever,
but then I would be hogging all the words.

OK. Now it's your turn to sing.